The Lost Necklace

Contents

Written by Susannah Reed

Illustrated by Dusan Pavlic

Collins

What's in this story?

Listen and say

Pirate Pat's Restaurant

milkshake

menu

fishing
boat

Bird Island

houseboats

river

Chapter 1: Everyone is hungry

It was a Saturday, after **football practice**.

"That was an exciting game!" said Daisy.

"Yes, it was great," said Jack. "But now I'm hungry."

"I'm very hungry!" said Fred, Daisy and Jack's little brother. "What shall we eat?"

"Let's go out for lunch," said Mum.

"Oh, yes please!" said Daisy.

"Let's go to Pirate Pat's," said Dad. "That's your favourite restaurant."

"Yay!" said Fred. "I love Pirate Pat's!"

"Me too," said Jack.

Pirate Pat's was a restaurant next to the river. It was the same shape as a pirate's ship and it had big windows. **Inside**, there were bowls of treasure on the tables.

The children sat at their favourite table. It was next to a big window.

The **weather** was good. The children could see the river and Bird Island.

Chapter 2: Daisy finds something

Jack and Fred looked at the menu.

"I'd like chicken noodles, please," said Fred, "and a tomato salad, too."

"And I'd like fish and chips, please," said Jack, "and a banana milkshake."

"Me too! Me too!" said Fred. "Banana milkshake is my favourite."

"What would you like, Daisy?" asked Jack. But Daisy didn't answer. She was under the table.

"What are you doing, Daisy?" asked Fred.

"There's **something** under this chair," said Daisy.

9

"It's a **necklace**!" said Daisy. "And look – these are letters. C, E, A, I and L. Ceail!"

"That's not a word!" said Fred.

"What does it mean?" said Daisy.

"I know," said Jack. "I think the letters spell a name."

"Look," said Jack, "L-A-I-C-E. No ... that's not a name. C-E-L-I-A: Celia! Celia is a girl's name. This necklace is hers."

"Oh, yes!" said Fred. "Well done, Jack."

"Let's find Celia," said Daisy. "Then we can give the necklace to her."

Chapter 3: Jack's good idea

"How can we find Celia?" asked Fred. "We don't know her."

"I've got an idea," said Jack. "Look at those drawings. They've all got names on them. Let's look for the name Celia."

"OK!" said Daisy. "We can try."

The children finished eating, then looked at the drawings. Jack smiled.

"I know that house!" said Daisy. "It's the square house on Bird Island. Let's go there!"

"Good idea!" said Jack. "We can go now with Uncle Joe. I can see him on his fishing boat."

"Mum, Dad, can we go to Bird Island with Uncle Joe?" asked Daisy.

"What, now?" said Mum. "Don't you want dessert?"

"OK, but go quickly," said Dad. "I'd like my dessert!"

Chapter 4: Off to Bird Island

The children ran to Uncle Joe's boat.

"Please can we come with you to Bird Island, Uncle Joe?" asked Jack.

"Yes, of course you can," said Uncle Joe. "Help me with these fish."

When they got to Bird Island, Uncle Joe **looked around**.

"Where can we put the boat?" he asked.

"There, Uncle Joe!" said Jack. "Put it next to that houseboat."

"It's a nice houseboat," said Daisy.

The children and Uncle Joe walked to the
square house and **knocked** on the door.
A girl opened it.

"We found your necklace. It was in Pirate Pat's restaurant, and ..." said Daisy. But then she stopped.

"You're wearing your necklace!" she said. "But then whose necklace is this?"

Celia looked at the necklace and smiled.

Chapter 5: Where's the houseboat?

"The letters on the necklace spell another name," Celia said. "Look!"

"Oh, yes!" said Jack. "A-L-I-C-E. Alice!"

"Alice is my cousin," Celia said. "We were in Pirate Pat's restaurant yesterday. This is her necklace."

"Alice lives on the island, too," said Celia. "We can go there with Mum and Dad."

"Does Alice live on a houseboat?" asked Daisy.

"Yes," said Celia. "How did you know?"

"I think I saw the houseboat," said Daisy. "Has it got flowers on it?"

They ran to the boats. They could see Joe's boat, but there was nothing next to it.

"Oh, no!" said Daisy. "Where's the houseboat?"

"It's there!" said Celia. "It's going to the town."

"Why is it going to town?" asked Jack.

"I think I know," said Celia.

"Me too," said Daisy. "Come on. We can all go in Uncle Joe's boat."

"Where are we going?" asked Fred.

"**Wait and see**!" said Daisy.

Chapter 6: Hello, Alice!

"There's the houseboat," said Daisy. "Look in the window."

"Oh, yes!" said Jack. "I can see the name, ALICE. That was clever, Daisy!"

"And there's Alice," said Celia. "She's **outside** Pirate Pat's."

The children got off the boat and ran to the restaurant.

"Alice!" Celia called.

Alice looked at them. She was very **surprised**.

"Hi Celia," she said. "What are *you* doing here?"

"We've got your necklace!" said Daisy.

"This is Daisy, Fred and Jack. They found the necklace in the restaurant," said Celia.

"Oh, thank you!" said Alice. "I **lost** the necklace yesterday."

"We know!" said Fred.

"Would you like to come and have dessert with us?" asked Daisy. "Our parents are **waiting** inside."

"Yes, please!" said Celia and Alice. "Pirate Pat's is our favourite restaurant."

"It's our favourite, too," said Jack happily. "I love banana milkshake."

Chapter 7: Dessert at Pirate Pat's

There was chocolate cake, ice cream and fruit salad. Everyone was happy and they started to eat. But then Fred stopped. He pointed under the window.

"What's that?" he asked.

Fred moved to the window and picked something up.

"What is it, Fred?" asked Jack.

"It's someone's bag," said Fred.

"Oh, no, not again!" said Daisy. "Let's finish our desserts **first**!"

Mini-dictionary

Listen and read

first (adverb) If you do something **first**, you do it before you do anything else.

football practice (noun) **Football practice** is when you play football often in order to be able to play better.

inside (adverb) If you are **inside** a place, you are in it.

knock (verb) If you **knock** on a door, you hit it to make a noise so someone knows you are there.

look around (phrasal verb) If you **look around**, you turn your eyes in different directions to see what is there.

lose (verb) If you have **lost** something, you do not know where it is.

outside (preposition) If you are **outside** a place, you are not in it but are very close to it.

something (pronoun) You use **something** to talk about a thing without saying exactly what it is.

surprised (adjective) If you are **surprised**, you did not expect something to happen.

wait (verb) If you **wait**, you spend time doing very little, before something happens.

wait and see (phrase) If you tell someone to "wait and see", you are saying that something exciting might be about to happen.

weather (noun) **Weather** is what it is like outside, for example if it is raining, hot or windy.

1 Look and order the story

2 Listen and say

Collins

Published by Collins
An imprint of HarperCollins*Publishers*
Westerhill Road
Bishopbriggs
Glasgow
G64 2QT

HarperCollins*Publishers*
1st Floor, Watermarque Building
Ringsend Road
Dublin 4
Ireland

William Collins' dream of knowledge for all began with the publication of his first book in 1819.

A self-educated mill worker, he not only enriched millions of lives, but also founded a flourishing publishing house. Today, staying true to this spirit, Collins books are packed with inspiration, innovation and practical expertise. They place you at the centre of a world of possibility and give you exactly what you need to explore it.

© HarperCollins*Publishers* Limited 2020

10 9 8 7 6 5 4 3 2

ISBN 978-0-00-839732-6

Collins® and COBUILD® are registered trademarks of HarperCollins*Publishers* Limited

www.collins.co.uk/elt

British Library Cataloguing in Publication Data

A catalogue record for this publication is available from the British Library.

Author: Susannah Reed
Illustrator: Dusan Pavlic (Beehive)
Series editor: Rebecca Adlard
Publishing manager: Lisa Todd
Product managers: Jennifer Hall and Caroline Green
In-house editor: Alma Puts Keren
Project manager: Emily Hooton
Editor: Matthew Hancock
Proofreaders: Natalie Murray and Michael Lamb
Cover designer: Kevin Robbins
Typesetter: 2Hoots Publishing Services Ltd
Audio produced by id audio, London
Reading guide author: Emma Wilkinson
Production controller: Rachel Weaver
Printed and bound by: GPS Group, Slovenia

Download the audio for this book and a reading guide for parents and teachers at www.collins.co.uk/839732